MINIONS: DRACULA'S LAST BIRTHDAY
A CENTUM BOOK 9781910114513

Published in Great Britain by Centum Books Ltd

This edition published 2015
2015 © Universal Studios Licensing LLC.

1 3 5 7 9 10 8 6 4 2

Centum Books Ltd, Unit 1, Upside Station Building, Solsbro Road, Torquay, Devon, UK, TQ2 6FD

books@centumbooksltd.co.uk

CENTUM BOOKS Limited Reg. No. 07641486

A CIP catalogue record for this book is available from the British Library

Printed in Italy

MINIONS

Dracula's Last Birthday

By Lucy Rosen
Illustrated by Ed Miller

centum

Minions have roamed the earth since the beginning of time. Before there was Gru, before there were evil gadgets to invent, before there were super villains who wanted to take over the world . . . there were Minions.

Ever since the very first Minion crawled out of the ocean and onto dry land, these little yellow creatures have been searching for one thing: the most terrible, wicked, despicable master they could find.

The Minions lived to serve.
They had no trouble tracking
down the biggest, baddest
dinosaur . . .

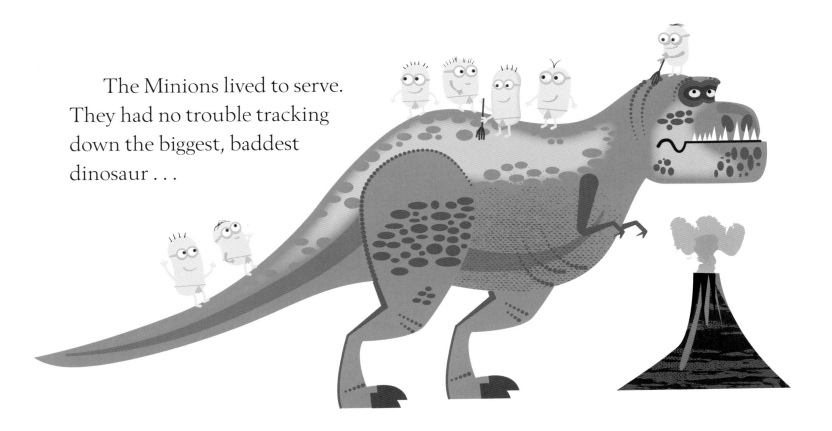

. . . or helping a wicked
pharaoh build a pyramid.

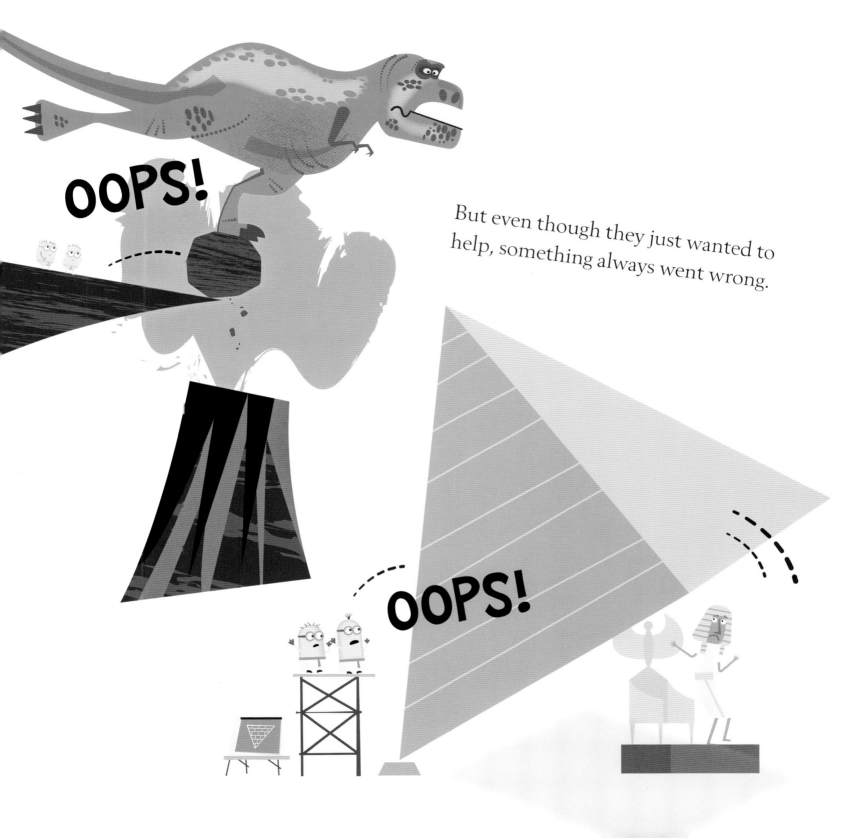

OOPS!

But even though they just wanted to help, something always went wrong.

OOPS!

Whenever disaster struck, the Minions kept moving. One day, they came across a dark stone castle. It looked creepy, creaky and cold. It was perfect! The Minions couldn't wait to meet whoever lived there.

The Minions pushed open the front door and peeked inside. Out of nowhere, bats came flying towards them!

"Oh, la no! Stopa, stopa!" they cried, trying to get away from the bat attack. The Minions tumbled into dusty cobwebs. They jumped into sticky cauldrons. They hid behind heavy, dirty curtains.

When the bats finally left, the Minions came out of their hiding spots and looked around. At the end of the long, dark hallway was a spooky wooden coffin. "Oooooh," they said.

One of the Minions walked up to the coffin. He knocked on the lid. It burst wide open. Dracula was inside!

"Velcome to my castle!" the evil vampire bellowed.

"Si, si, si!" cried the Minions. They couldn't believe it. They had found their new master!

"Big boss! Big boss! Big boss!" they cheered.

BIG BOSS!

The Minions got right to work trying to help Dracula however they could. First, they decided to clean up the castle. Carl and Mike took turns sweeping the cobwebs.

"Me do it," Carl said.

"No, me, me do it," Mike replied.

"Speta, me la do it," Carl insisted.

"Me!" said Mike.

"Me!" said Carl.

Soon enough, the two Minions were tussling down the hallway. They bounced and rolled and rumbled all around, until they got tangled up in an enormous web!

Next, the Minions replaced all of Dracula's melted candles. One by one, they removed the old wax. They carefully polished each candlestick. They gently put in fresh new candles.

Then they lit them all with a torch.

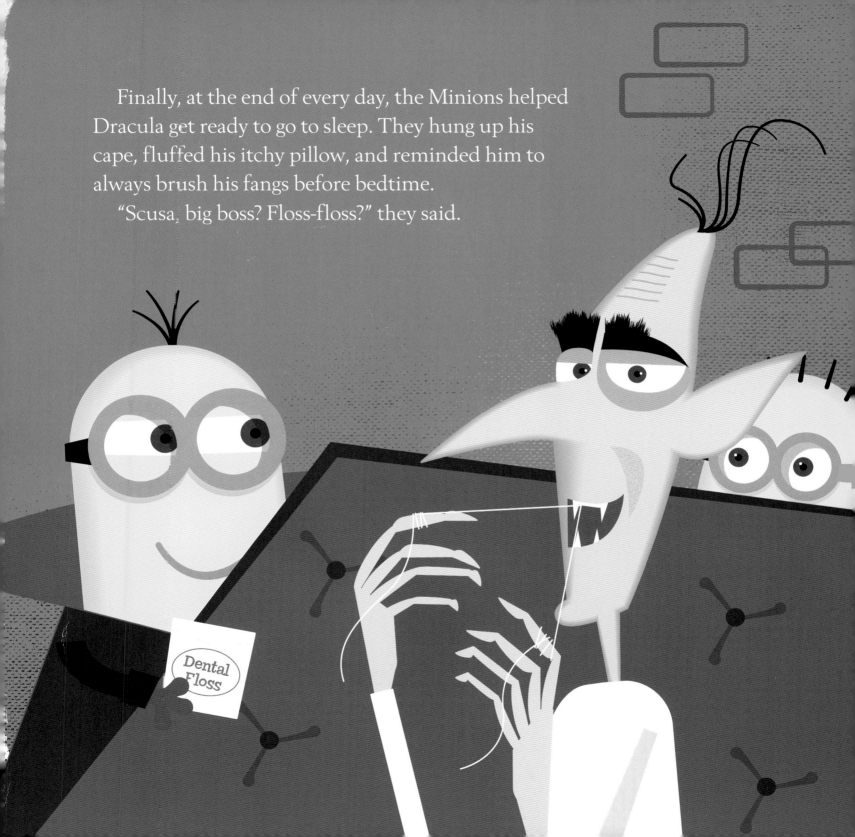

Finally, at the end of every day, the Minions helped Dracula get ready to go to sleep. They hung up his cape, fluffed his itchy pillow, and reminded him to always brush his fangs before bedtime.

"Scusa, big boss? Floss-floss?" they said.

Dental Floss

Over time, Dracula came to rely on the Minions and think of them as his friends. He even let them in on a secret.

"Tomorrow vill be my three-hundred-und-fifty-seventh birthday!" he said proudly.

October

DRACULA'S BIRTHDAY!

31

October

30

The Minions were excited. They wanted to throw their evil boss an evil party to celebrate his many years of evil-doing. But they didn't have much time.

Kevin made a list of all the things they'd need to do: Bake a cake. Make drinks. Find a great gift . . .

Dave and Paul got started on the cake. They mixed together eggs, flour, strawberries and sugar. "Yum, yum," they said.

SUGAR

FLOUR

Chuck and Norbert made punch in one of Dracula's cauldrons. They put ice cream and fresh fruit in the juice. Delicious!

Finding the right gift was the hardest part. What does a Minion get for the villain who has it all? The Minions put their heads together until they thought of the perfect present: a portrait of Dracula with all his yellow friends by his side.

They got to work painting their masterpiece.

Finally, it was time! The big day had arrived. Dave and Paul led Dracula to the ballroom, where the party was just getting started.

"Surprise!" the Minions yelled.

"Ah, how vonderful!" Dracula cackled as he sipped from his goblet of fruit punch.

"Big boss, big cake," said Kevin. He opened the door to reveal Minions carrying a strawberries and cream cake.

Dracula took a deep breath and blew out the candles.

They were about to give Dracula his present when Norbert realised it was too dark to see. They had gone to a lot of trouble making it perfect, and he wanted to make sure their boss would enjoy it.

"Le idea!" Kevin said.

The Minions grabbed the curtains and pulled them apart. Sunlight poured in and onto their painting.

"Paratu, big boss!" the Minions cooed, admiring their work of art.

Dracula didn't reply.

"Big boss?" they said.

Dracula did not say a word.

The Minions turned around.

Where Dracula had been sitting, there was now a big pile of ashes. The Minions forgot about the vampire's biggest weakness: sunlight!

"Uh, no," said Stuart, slapping his forehead. "Not again."

Another evil boss,
another Minion accident.
The little yellow creatures
sighed and moved on.

Soon, they found another perfect despicable master in a French captain. At least – that is – until they messed up again.

OOPS!